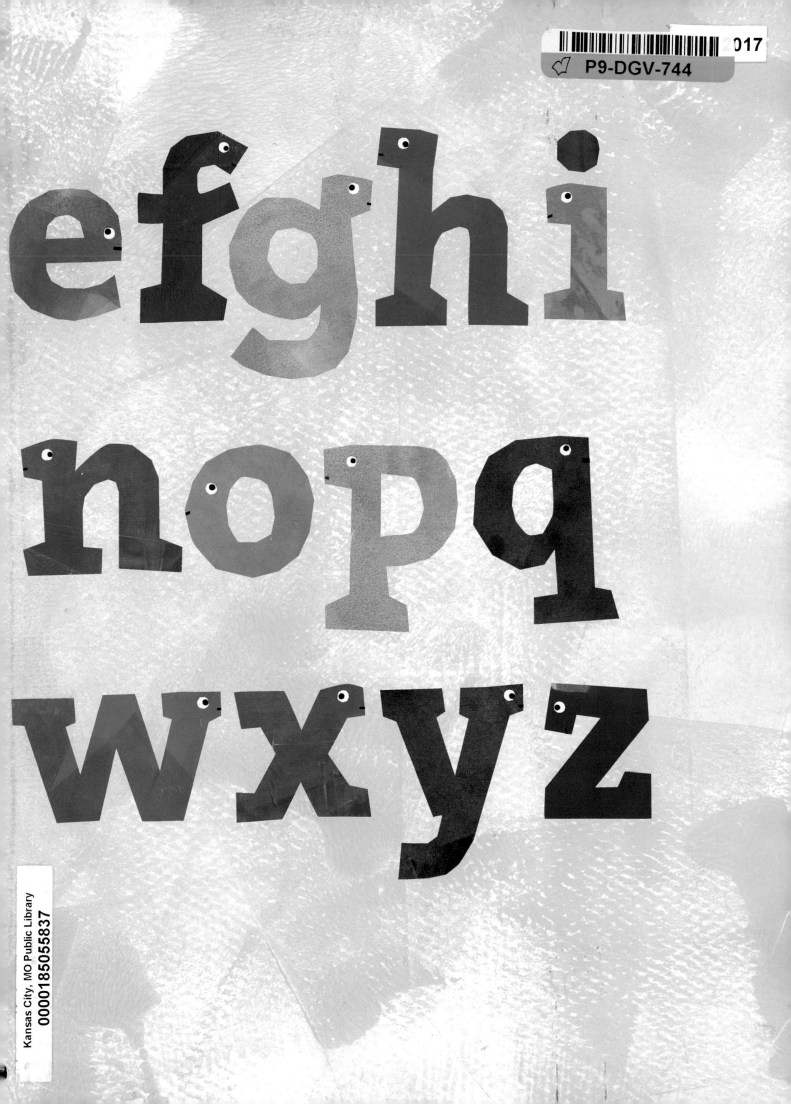

Little i
Michael Hall

For Susan, Sarah, and Jamie

Little i. Copyright © 2017 by Michael Hall. All rights reserved. Manufactured in China. For information address HarperCollins Children's Books, a division of HarperCollins Publishers, 195 Broadway, New York, NY 10007. www.harpercollinschildrens.com. The art consists of digitally combined collages of painted and cut paper. The text type is 24-point TheSerifB W4 SemiLight. Library of Congress Cataloging-in-Publication Data is available.   ISBN 978-0-06-238300-6 (hardback)   17 18 19 20 21 SCP 10 9 8 7 6 5 4 3 2 1

First Edition

Greenwillow Books
An Imprint of HarperCollinsPublishers

When
Little i's
dot
fell off,

rolled
down
a hill,

tumbled
over
a cliff,

and
splashed
into the
sea,

the alphabet was confused.
Without a dot,
Little i looked like a number.
It was odd.

"strange," said s, t, r, a, n, g, and e.

And you can't make any words
with a number.

"no way!" said n and o,
and w, a, and y.

Where was the dot?
Little i set out to find it.

"best of luck!"
said b, e, s, and t,
and o and f,
and l, u, c, and k.

Little i searched the sea for weeks.
Was the dot there? It was not there.
But Little i did not give up.

Little i landed on an island
and walked along
a winding seaside passage
that went all the way
from one end
to the other.

Was the dot there? It was not there.
But Little i saw something. . . .

It was
exciting!
Spectacular!
Magnificent!

And very,
very loud!

Little i explored a cold, dark tunnel.
Was the dot there?

It was not there.
(But Little i discovered precious gems
sparkling in the walls.)

The garden of sprouts was lovely.
Was the dot there? It was not there.

But Little i paused, paused,
and paused again, to admire each one.

Little i hiked up a hill,
climbed down several steps,
crossed a spine-chilling bridge,
and rambled on and on and on,
all the way to the end
of the winding seaside passage.

Was the dot there?

Yes. It was!
Little i stopped.
At last.

But now,
oddly,
the dot
felt
awkward.

It
wouldn't
stay in
its place.

And
what's more,
Little i had
grown
to like
being
dotless.

So,
very gently,
Little i
put the dot
back in its
new spot,

and headed home without it.

And one day . . .
"ahoy!"
said a, h, o, and y.

The alphabet was silent
as Little i approached.

Was the dot there?
It was not there.
And Little i had changed.
Little i wasn't little anymore.

What had Little i become?

A word!
"I," said Big I!

"bravo!" said b, r, a, v, and o.
And with that, the entire alphabet cheered.

Question
Mark
Boat

Winding
Seaside
Passage

Spectacular
Exclamation
Point
Waterfall

Cold, Dark
Parenthesis
Tunnel*

*(With
Sparkling
Asterisk
Gems)

Lovely
Comma
Sprouts

Little i's Island